Gallery Books
Editor: Peter Fallon

THE SANCTUARY LAMP

Thomas Murphy

The Sanctuary Lamp

A revision

 Gallery Books

This revised edition is
first published simultaneously
in paperback and in a cloth-
bound edition in 1984.

The Gallery Press
19 Oakdown Road
Dublin 14. Ireland.

© Thomas Murphy 1976, 1984

All rights reserved

Cover design by Michael Kane

ISBN 0 904011 54 2 (*paper*)
      0 904011 55 0 (*cloth*)

All performing rights in this play are strictly reserved. Applications for
amateur productions must be made in advance to The Gallery Press and for
professional productions to Frazer & Dunlop Ltd., 91 Regent Street, London
W1R 8RU or Ms. B. Aschenberg, ICM, 40 West 5th Street, N.Y. 10019.
The Gallery Press receives financial assistance from The Arts Council/An
Chomhairle Ealaíon, Ireland.

To Noel and Mary, Murt and Dorothy,
Vincent and Patsy, Fergal and Brid,
Andy and ?

Characters

Harry
Monsignor
Maudie
Francisco

A church in a city.

Introductory and bridging music from 'The Sleeping Beauty'.

ACT ONE

SCENE ONE

A church. Late afternoon light filtering through a stained-glass window—the window depicting the Holy Family; great columns to dwarf the human form; a pulpit; a statue of Jesus; a confessional tucked away somewhere; and a lamp, the sanctuary lamp, in a brass container suspended from the ceiling. (Other features as required, as benefits director's/designer's ideas. The sacristy and vestry mentioned later are assumed to be off.)

HARRY is seated hunched in a pew. He is in his forties; unshaven; we recognise him as a down-and-out; his rumpled suit/overcoat, though the worse for wear, gives some indication of his childish vanity and reflect former better years. And an affectation in his sound ('y'know?' 'old boy' etc.—British officer type) but it started a long time ago and is now part of his personality.

An elderly priest, a MONSIGNOR, *is pacing slowly up and down reading a book. A touch of cynicism (his recurring invitatory short laugh: 'What?'), disillusioned, but a very humane man.*

And MAUDIE, *whom we see later, is sixteen; a waif-like thing about her.*

HARRY is now considering MONSIGNOR; *he coughs, raises his hand tentatively, coughs, to get Monsignor's attention.* MONSIGNOR *looks enquiringly at him.*

HARRY	Y'know!
MONSIGNOR	Hmm?
HARRY	Excuse, but, Padre—is it? Padre? Padre?—Is there anything you can suggest?
MONSIGNOR	Hmm?
HARRY	Quite frankly I'm intelligent, I'm a very strong man, and you may think it a paradox but I do not know how to get out of the puzzle I am in.
MONSIGNOR	Yes?
HARRY	Excuse my butting in because I can see you are—y'know?—but something on my mind, dire need of help and I'm not talking about soup.
MONSIGNOR	(*Considering* HARRY) Hum, hum, haa. There's just a chance that . . . What's y'r name?
HARRY	Harry, sir—Padre—Henry.
MONSIGNOR	Harry?
HARRY	Sol'min.

MONSIGNOR I see. And what've y'been doing with yourself then, Harry?

HARRY Well, actually, it's not quite that.

MONSIGNOR Hmm?

HARRY Well, casual work, actually—if you must know. And very occasional casual work recently. And begging, frankly.

MONSIGNOR I see.

HARRY But it's not quite that. This compulsion to do this terrible thing.

MONSIGNOR Yes?

HARRY But I didn't do it.

MONSIGNOR Good ——

HARRY No.

MONSIGNOR Yes?

HARRY The compulsion is there to go back and do it now. And a feeling of wrong-doing because I haven't gone back to do it. A terrible deed! So what am I to do?

MONSIGNOR Yes?

HARRY (*Surprised/confused by* MONSIGNOR'S *seeming blandness*) What? . . . To get the question straight. But, demoralisation—y'know? Deterioration—y'know? And worse, more confused by it all by the day.

MONSIGNOR What business were you in, Harry?

HARRY What?

MONSIGNOR What has led to your—present circumstances?

HARRY The financial side?

MONSIGNOR If you like.

HARRY Well, though not very important as I said, they never stamped my cards—y'see?—and that's difficult to explain at the Labour Exchange.

MONSIGNOR I see. And who are 'they'?

HARRY In the circus. I was the strong man.

MONSIGNOR Were you indeed? Fancy that!

HARRY Oh yes. But when there was a general cutting-down on things, when it became unviable—y'know? Unviable?—to feed the larger animals, they asked me to muck in with this act. Me, Francisco, Olga, and the dwarf. Contortionist, Olga, actually. Getting herself into distress. It wasn't circus.

MONSIGNOR So you left?

HARRY (*Hedging*) Well I . . . Hmm?

MONSIGNOR So you packed it in?

HARRY Ah—Hmm?

MONSIGNOR Hum, hum, haa!

HARRY Would you like me to tell the truth? (*A single slow nod of the head from* MONSIGNOR) Well, when we'd have done our act we were obliged to wait around for the grand finale. Quite a bit of time to kill, actually, because we did not top the bill. And I did not think it was proper for Francisco and Olga to spend that time alone. So we spent it all together. And Francisco—not Italian, not Spanish, a juggler, actually—has this interest, great interest in religion—holy religion? Mind you, so do I. The Gentiles—y'know? Holy Gentiles? Anyways, quite a bit of time to kill, all together, all quite correct, until one night the subject of holy religion comes up and . . . (*He hesitates*)

MONSIGNOR A row broke out. (*He chuckles*)

HARRY Well, just three blows, bum—bum—bum, one for each of them.

MONSIGNOR And you got the sack?

HARRY (*Chuckles with* MONSIGNOR) Indeed. Indeed.

MONSIGNOR Yes?

HARRY Oh, but we still stayed together.

MONSIGNOR Yes?

HARRY Went—y'know?—went freelance? Quite adventurous, mind you, some of the engagements we got but . . .

MONSIGNOR Yes?

HARRY Not very ennobling.

MONSIGNOR I see. Anything else?

HARRY Ahm. (*He still wants to talk about his 'compulsion'. He changes his mind*) You were going to say, Padre?

MONSIGNOR Well, as it happens, our clerk died three weeks ago last Wednesday. The bishop sends around one of his young priests occasionally to help out. With a guitar. But no replacement for old Bill. Otherwise I should not be here at two o'clock in the day reading Hermann Hesse, what? I should be at home by my fireside reading Hermann Hesse. D'ja read, Harry?

HARRY Oh yes.

MONSIGNOR Lovely stuff. I don't know how I've missed out on him for so long. But as to the job of Clerk here, it's yours as far as I'm concerned, if you're interested.

HARRY Job?

MONSIGNOR (*He is searching his pocket and producing an envelope which he uses as a bookmarker*) Actually causes me physical pain to turn down the corner of a page.

11

Ridiculous, what? (HARRY *shifts a little. He has not expected this offer*) You're not sure?

HARRY   Not quite that—y'know?—but . . . Job!

MONSIGNOR   Hmm?

HARRY   Clerk?

MONSIGNOR   Oh! Silly sort of name for it, really. No, the sort of thing that if someone comes along and wants a Mass said, you write in the diary Mass for N on such-and-such a day, Baptismal Cert for so-and-so. I'd hardly call it clerking. Soon get used to it, soon get bored by it.

HARRY   Padre.

MONSIGNOR   Your duties, mainly, would be to do with . . . (*He glances at* MAUDIE *who has entered to cross the background, glance shiftily at them and exit*) To do with keeping an eye on the place. Locking up at night before you go home, and opening up again in the morning. Okay?

HARRY   Padre.

MONSIGNOR   Pay's not much, I'm afraid—Are you married?

HARRY   No.

MONSIGNOR   Hmm?

HARRY   Y'know?

MONSIGNOR   Twenty-nine pounds a week. Let me show you around. Ridiculous, I suppose, in this day and age, but, there you are. This is the Vestry. Sort of my domain. And over here is the Sacristy. Soutane is supplied, second-hand but dry-cleaned and that, and who knows but it may have been the bishop's. What? D'ja know him? The bishop?

HARRY   No.

MONSIGNOR   And this is the Sacristy, sort of your domain, your kitchen so to speak. D'ja know him to see?

HARRY   Indeed.

MONSIGNOR   Yes. Little gas-ring in there for your elevenses. That sort of thing. Please ask any questions. And that confessional over there: old Bill, your predecessor— if you decide to take the job—old Bill used it for the brooms and things. Yes?

HARRY   W.C. in there?

MONSIGNOR   Yes. And you have your hand-basin over there. (HARRY *nods thoughtfully* . . . Hmm?

HARRY   Nightwatchman?

MONSIGNOR   No. You would have to see that everything is securely

	locked up before leaving each night.
HARRY	(*Reflectively*) Very handy.
MONSIGNOR	Okay?
HARRY	Padre.
MONSIGNOR	Oh, by the way, I'm a Monsignor. Silly sort of title really, but, there you are. Okay?
HARRY	Okay.
MONSIGNOR	And this of course is the Sanctuary Lamp.
HARRY	First thing I noticed.
MONSIGNOR	Signifying the constant Presence.
HARRY	It's a mystery I suppose.
MONSIGNOR	I suppose it is. Despite all the recent innovation this still needs personal attention, so you would be required to replace the candle every twenty-four hours.
HARRY	It shouldn't go out. (*Eyes fixed on lamp*) First thing I noticed. (MONSIGNOR *looks at him*) And the silence. I'll accept the position.
MONSIGNOR	You're clear on what has to be done?
HARRY	Leave it to me.
MONSIGNOR	Splendid. Well let me take your address. Formality for the bishop's office. (*Poised to write in his diary*) Yes?
HARRY	Certainly.
MONSIGNOR	Yes?
HARRY	22 Paxton Street.
MONSIGNOR	(*Writing*) Paxton Street. Very good. (*He glances at his book as if eager to be away*)
HARRY	Though, mind you, I won't be very often in.
MONSIGNOR	No. Very good, any other? (*Questions*)
HARRY	Do I—? (*He mimes pulling a bellrope*)
MONSIGNOR	No. That one's alright. Electronics, what?
HARRY	Monsignor.
MONSIGNOR	Splendid. (*Both are pleased with themselves.* MONSIGNOR *is looking around to see what next to show to* HARRY) I do wish the wages were a bit better, but—Well, let's see how you get on. Let's see now. Yes. (*He is about to lead* HARRY *off when he gets a sudden thought*) Oh, by the way, you are a Catholic, aren't you? (*They are looking at each other: mutual dismay beginning to appear.* HARRY *gives a single nod, hopefully in the affirmative*) . . . What's the most dangerous animal in the circus?
HARRY	The horse, actually.

MONSIGNOR *gives a slow single nod. Then, leading* HARRY *off, as the lights change and bridging music comes up.*

MONSIGNOR The switches for the lights are down here . . .

And MAUDIE *is entering, to stand there looking after them, as the lights fade to nothing.*

SCENE TWO

Night. HARRY *now dressed in a soutane is standing in the pulpit to inspect the pendant sanctuary lamp the better: the old candle does not yet need to be replaced. He sighs. The church clock starts to chime ten. He begins to feel the church and the night closing in on him.*

HARRY What is it, my soul, already?

He comes down from the pulpit, pauses to consider the trunk-like base of the pulpit . . . Next, he faces the empty church, flexes his muscles and calls:

All out!

Then into action, exiting and entering with a large bunch of keys locking doors. Then he extinguishes the lights and the sanctuary lamp comes more dramatically into relief. In the unaccustomed dark HARRY *bumps into something and growls; he bumps into something else and he emits a growl of rage as he pulls off his soutane and squares up to the pulpit. To the lamp*

See! See!

He tries to lift the pulpit and fails. To the lamp

Why do you resent me? . . . And being watched here as no servant—as no menial!—was ever watched before. I have every right to be here! (*Then to himself, selecting a key from his large key-ring*) Every right. I thought he'd be back to lock up with me. But then

14

he may show up yet. So —— (*He pockets the selected key*) Y'see? That's okay. (*His purpose beginning to falter, dismally*) I'd be as well off in the park again tonight . . . (*Addressing the lamp again*) I won't be staying here for nothing! . . . You get nothing for nothing, that's business, isn't it? Well, then. So I'll bung a deuce of quids into (St.) Anthony's box every Friday . . . y'know? . . . And we're all God's children, whatever religion . . . (*He begins to feel he may have misinterpreted the lamp*) Of course it's not a question of the money with you either. Or—— (*He imitates the whispering sound he has heared people make when praying*) What? Like calling a cat! (*He moves slowly circling the lamp, then sits looking at it*) The silence turns to loneliness, Jesus? Time passing . . . My spirit is unwell too. They've been trying to crush my life. They even had me wrestling with a dwarf—with Sam, y'know?—and he had to win. I don't mind being a clown but I'm not a fool. So, supposing we can come to some arrangement, I have every confidence I can get well here. Supposing in exchange for the accommodation I engage to make good conversation—break the back of night for you? (*To himself*) Alleviate the holy loneliness. (*To the lamp*) But there would have to be a time limit. Supposing I say till two a.m.? Till three? What's a fair time? Till three is generous, and by my reckoning that will be about the time to replace the candle. I wish he'd told me the proper time to do it. So that's settled then. What shall we talk about? . . . Not a very busy one today, Jesus? No. Not a very busy one. Or tonight? No . . . You know Francisco? Juggler actually. Well, he was my friend, I took him in. Then he usurped, sneaked my wife. And now he lives— my greatest friend!—quite openly with her. And we had brought a child into the world . . . I wouldn't have let a thing like that go by a few years ago. (*He looks at the pulpit*) And I'd have waltzed around the room with that. (*He retrieves his soutane*) Do you think madness must at least be warm? I don't mind telling you I keep it as a standby in case all else fails. (*He suspends the action of putting on the soutane*) You never feel your soul when you're happy. (*He starts to dance for some moments, movements vaguely balletic and reminiscent of a child's. Then*) And sometimes, in the

15

mornings actually, she'd toddle up to my bunk, toddle up to my bunk, bright little eyes—very bright, mind you—arms tightly round my—(*neck*), and laughing, laughing, admiring her daddy—y'know? y'know?—admiring her daddy. Teresa. (*A noise off. He listens. Silence. He continues to button his soutane*) I was very famous too. And always careful of my dress. (*He sits*) The Duke of Windsor, he was a well-dressed man. Knew him—David, y'know?—first names, David, very chaming. (*The clock chimes the half hour. He rises as if having somewhere to go. Impotence, nowhere to go and he sits again*) Only half-ten . . . Oh, but I have every confidence of our little arrangement proving mutually fruitful, so let me think again . . . (*Then, growing animated, he rises suddenly*) But-if-I-stop-to-think-I-only-start-to-think of my daughter-daughter-daughter, Teresa! No one to feed the wonder in the eyes of a child. Help me to forget! You who rule the heavens and the earth, stretch forth your mighty arms therefore: help me to forget. (*He sits*) And once out walking, and a shower of rain, and no other shelter, so naturally I put her under my jersey. Like a little bird nestling—I could even feel her heart—and she even fell asleep there. Frankly proud of that. But then I'd think of the years ahead and people like myself already laying traps, and then I'd look into her eyes and I'd feel I must cry, or my breastbone must certainly snap in two. (*Another creak off. He listens. Then he forgets it*) You know Olga? Wife actually, Olga. Well she was very lonely. And she seemed—y'know? Superior?—ladylike type of person. Told me she'd been a ballerina once. (*She*) May have been daydreaming, of course. And I was one of the best sports, so we became married. And we had Teresa. Then she started to say, look at you, you disgust me, just look at you. And, when I tried to swop the lonely thoughts of the small hours with her, that I bored her actually. Olga. Real name was Winifred of course. And then Francisco sneaked her. Then she started to say, 'People!'—Like that—'People! . . . Then, me in the bunk, Teresa in the cot, eyes open to the night, through the night, every night. As if no one else in all the world. Time passing. As if no one else in all . . . space. In silhouette—that's it,

that's it, in silhouette. Little girl and a man, standing
black on the edge of the world, the edge of it all,
looking out at all the sad, slow-moving mists of time
and space. And me such a strong man and could do
nothing. (*Suddenly*) Where do you go when you die?
. . . I made some attempt to alleviate of course, and
after lights-out pretended to teach her some tables. Up
to seven times. Just in case she understood. And little
lectures on history. Italy—y'know? I was there. But
there are limits to tables and lectures on history, and
eventually I'd say 'night-night'—y'know? 'Night-
night'—and wait. Then just the occasional—(*He mimics
the double-beated cough of a child*) Just the occasional
—(*He repeats the cough*) to punctuate, time passing
. . . Of course all this time Olga was off, having
herself screwed, panting for unhappy life in the very
next room. With Francisco. Or making love to all
and sundry. Nothing could flower . . . Then always
there would come a point: time passing would stop—
and this terrible thing come knocking at my heart.
Keeps knocking at my heart. But I kept on hesitating.
Night after night this thought would come: well, if
as they say there is no law, there is no God, mustn't
I take charge? . . . Once I did get up, penknife opened,
pounding heart, I thought I'll do it now. Nothing on
my daughter's face to urge me to kill them. Still, I
thought, I'll do it now. Then looked into their room.
Nothing but a burning light of hatred—Invitation!
—from the darkness from their eyes. Then I'd say
if I was mad I'd do it. If I was mad I'd hurry back
and do it now. But I do not want to be like them,
I believe in life! And I kept on hesitating till all
I could do was lie there with the child. Because
no one should be on their own. It's even bad for a
dog . . . And then of course she died. But very interesting—I was very surprised—all I could do was say
what does it matter, and left. Well, I waited till we
got our next engagement—quite an important engagement actually, I wonder how it went? And to punish
them, I walked away. Well, sloped, actually, to let
them down. (*He pauses: the awareness of the inad-
equacy of his retaliation makes him stand suddenly in
frustration. He starts to lurch at the pulpit*) I *sloped*
away! (*He checks himself. Then, intensely*) Oh, Lord

17

of Death, I cannot forget! Oh Lord of Death, don't let me forget! Oh Lord of Death, stretch forth your mighty arms, therefore! Stir, move, rouse yourself to strengthen me and I'll punish them properly this time! (*A noise off that sounds like a sob. He listens. Silence*) Every confidence. (*He listens again. Silence*) Still, I wonder how that last engagement went. Isn't that surprising? (*A creak off. He listens. Another creak.* HARRY *is motionless. He thinks it is* FRANCISCO. *He takes out a penknife and opens it. Whispers*) Ah, very shrewd Francisco, very cunning. (*To lamp*) Thank you. (*Loudly*) Ah—excuse for just a moment. (*He exits*)

MAUDIE *is entering cautiously. A light is switched on revealing her fully, her tear-stained face, her fear, and* HARRY *is entering with his penknife. The sight of her stops him.*

HARRY   What are you doing here, Miss?—Don't scream! . . . What is the meaning of—y'know?

MAUDIE   You frightened me.

HARRY   What?

MAUDIE   You frightened me.

HARRY   Did you come here to burgle?

MAUDIE   I was here first.

HARRY   What? You don't work here! This pad goes with the job. Yes it does! (*She runs: he intercepts her*) How long has this carry-on been going on? (*She starts to cry*) Tears to no avail! . . . Shh! . . . Haven't you nowhere else to go? . . . Shh! . . . There, there now . . . There, there now . . . y'know? . . . Are you hungry? . . . Don't move. (*Gets his jacket from which he produces two slices of fruit cake wrapped in paper. He offers her a slice of the bread*) Would you like a slice of—? . . . Stoller. Fruit cake . . . Time was when stoller was the only sweetmeat I allowed myself. (*Offering bread again*) Hmm? . . . And I was a great believer in liver, raw eggs, brown bread and yogurt . . . Hmm?

MAUDIE   (*Accepts*) Ta.

HARRY   Y'see? I thought you might be hungry. I always kept myself well. What's your name?

MAUDIE   Maudie.

HARRY   What?

MAUDIE   *Mau*-die.

HARRY   That's a very nice— y'know? Very charming . . . Why are you dossing here, Maudie? (MAUDIE *is unforthcoming*) And I was always proud of my lightness of step. Many people commented on it . . . Alright?

MAUDIE   Cold.

HARRY   (*Looks at his jacket*) Actually, this has got a slight odour about it.

MAUDIE   There are cloaks in there.

HARRY   Hang about. (HARRY *exits to the vestry and returns with a vestment which he puts on her*) Y'see? . . . Hmm?

MAUDIE   Who else is here?

HARRY   No need to be frightened. The Presence.

MAUDIE   Jesus?

HARRY   Not quite. Well, it's his spirit actually. They nabbed his spirit and they've got it here. It's a mystery of course but that's what religion is. (*She looks at him*) Personally, I think they should let him go but, there you are.

MAUDIE   (*Indicating statue*) That's Jesus, isn't it?

HARRY   That's Jesus . . . Do you adore him?

MAUDIE   (*Looks at him*) Do you?

HARRY   No. Y'know?

MAUDIE   Neither do I.

HARRY   I've great respect for him, mind you.

MAUDIE   He gives forgiveness.

HARRY   A very high regard. A veritable giant of a man, if you want my opinion, but between one thing and another, his sense is gone a little dim. And who would blame him? Locked up here at night, reclining—y'know?— reflecting his former glory. So a bit of diversion helps.

MAUDIE   But he gives forgiveness.

HARRY   (*Sharply/defensively*) How do you know? He doesn't have to forgive me. I did nothing wrong. I don't reproach myself. So, y'see? You have to commit the sin first to get that. But, properly approached, of course, he can still do other things. Would you care to— (*Sit*)?

MAUDIE   And he likes children, doesn't he?

HARRY   (*Looks at her for a moment*) Well, of course he does. In the holy booklets down there: *Suffer the little children to come to me.*

MAUDIE   Ay?

HARRY   Hmm?

MAUDIE	Suffering?
HARRY	No. Suffer. Suffer, in our parlance means, please allow. Please allow the little ones to come to me' that's what he used to say.
MAUDIE	. . . Are you a priest?
HARRY	Not quite.
MAUDIE	(*First smile—a shy innocent smile—from* MAUDIE) I didn't think you were.
HARRY	I'm the clerk. Assistant monsignor, y'know. Silly sort of title really but, there you are.
MAUDIE	Who's that then?
HARRY	Joseph, y'know? Mary's spouse, Joseph. I've always had a soft spot for Joseph. I've always felt he must have been a bit lonely. Though, mind you, there's some that say she had other children. Quite a large family of them in it, I've heard a person say, so, maybe one of them had a bit of time for him. Joseph. I've always taken an interest.
MAUDIE	No, who's the little boy.
HARRY	Oh! That's the Infant.
MAUDIE	He's my favourite.
HARRY	Not mine. I'm quite fond of children, actually, but he's too clever-looking by half for me.
MAUDIE	I like him best.
HARRY	What does your mam and dad think about your staying out at night like this? . . . Do they punish you? Do they beat you? (MAUDIE *shakes her head*) What?
MAUDIE	Grandad.
HARRY	Do you stay with your grandad? (*She nods*) Hmm?
MAUDIE	And gran.
HARRY	And do they punish you? (*She nods*) For staying out? (*Sho looks at him*) Is that why you don't go home? (*It's not the reason: she doesn't want to talk. She averts her eyes*) . . . I haven't much time for her either. Mary. It was a good idea alright: holy family— y'know?—the three of them. But see that expression of hers? I know someone like that. And she was a Catholic too. But of course it was all a front to conceal a very highly-strung neurotic nymphomaniac. Where's your dad, Maudie? (MAUDIE *gives the slightest shrug*) Where's your mam? (MAUDIE *is unforthcoming*) Are you still hungry? (*She nods*)

20

The clock chimes eleven.

MAUDIE   And tired.

HARRY   But, we don't want to turn in yet. It's only— (*Eleven o'clock*) A bit of diversion—conversation—And made a promise to replace the— Here, I only need a little piece of this. The smallest piece of food in the stomach prevents an ulcer. (*He gives her the major portion of the other slice of bread*)

MAUDIE   Ta.

HARRY   Y'see?

MAUDIE   Are you going to send me home?

HARRY   (*Disappointed*) When?

MAUDIE   Tomorrow.

HARRY   But I didn't think you'd want to.

MAUDIE   I won't want to.

HARRY   Well then. (*She smiles*) But we'll have to be careful. (*She agrees. Both are pleased. A few surreptitious glances at* HARRY *and* MAUDIE *decides to talk*)

MAUDIE   Do you know John Wayne?

HARRY   Indeed.

MAUDIE   . . . Not personally.

HARRY   Ah . . . No. No, I know quite a few of that—elite, y'know?—but not John Wayne.

MAUDIE   Well, he is one of grandad's favourite heroes.

HARRY   Oh yes?

MAUDIE   (*Nods*) Well, one night he weren't much use, and grandad come home, sad, with gran, from the ABC.

HARRY   They were unfulfilled.

MAUDIE   Sad.

HARRY   Oh yes?

MAUDIE   And I were standing at our gate and didn't see in time. And grandad gave me a hiding. Because I'd put my foot outside the door. And then he put his boot to the telly. Because it were snowing. And the telly-man said it were no accident, and grandad had to pay. And grandad said he'd have no telly in the house again, even if it were to choke him.

HARRY   Black and white?

MAUDIE   . . . What?

HARRY   The telly.

MAUDIE   Yes.

HARRY   But why weren't you meant to put your foot outside the door?

21

MAUDIE . . . What?

HARRY You're—y'know?—big girl . . . Where's your mam?

MAUDIE *My* mam? (*He nods*) *My* mam is dead.

HARRY Oh . . . When did she . . .?

MAUDIE When did she die? (*She smiles*) I think it were a few
years ago.

HARRY Oh yes?

MAUDIE Well, do you know 'dreaming'?

HARRY Oh yes?

MAUDIE Do you?

HARRY Indeed.

MAUDIE Well, I don't know. I never saw my mam. Not that
I remember. I saw my dad alright, but I never saw
my mam. They went their separate ways, gran said.
Well, (a) few years ago, I started to—dream—about
my mam. Then I knew she were dead. But I think
she were really visiting me. But gran said, dreaming.
But I don't agree. But gran said 'dreaming, Maudie,
dreaming' and not to be dementing her and not let
grandad hear. (*She looks at* HARRY *for his appraisal*)

HARRY Oh yes?

MAUDIE Well, grandad heard and said I were a whore's melt.
And gran said then I were a millstone. (*She smiles at*
HARRY)

Note: To MAUDIE, *this story is essentially one of
personal triumph.*

HARRY Oh yes?

MAUDIE Well, do you know 'in bed'?

HARRY At night?

MAUDIE Yes. Her face would come beside me, in the dark, like
a plate. And her eyes would look at me. And I didn't
know what to say. So then I'd look about for gran.
Or even grandad. To say something. But when I'd
look around again, my mam were always gone. And
then I'd try to scream. To fill the room again. But I
couldn't scream. And it went on like that. Like, every
night. Like, forever. (HARRY *nods*) Well, one night, I
knew there were a change. She were not staring at me
any more. She were looking down. More peaceful.
Like reading the paper. Or thinking it out. And I
looked about to see if gran had seen this change for
the better. Gran had seen alright, but she wouldn't

pretend. And I knew that when I'd look around again my mam would still be there. And she were. And I waited. But then my mam got up— (MAUDIE *gives a haughty toss of her hair*) My mam got up and went out. I were so disappointed. I think I were going to cry. But then the door opened again and my mam were standing there, and she looked at no one else, and she said, 'Oh by the way, Maudie, I'm very happy now.' And I were so grateful. And then I told my gran, whether it were dreaming or not, it were all over.

HARRY And what did your gran say?

MAUDIE She said it were forgiveness. (MAUDIE *smiles her personal triumph and* HARRY *complements*)

HARRY (*To sanctuary lamp*) That was very successful. That was very—y'know? But why do they punish you now?

MAUDIE . . . What?

HARRY Y'know?

MAUDIE . . . Do you know 'lamp-posts'?

HARRY In the street?

MAUDIE Yes.

HARRY Oh yes?

MAUDIE Well, there's one outside our house, and I've been able to climb it since I was eight.

HARRY No ropes attached?

MAUDIE No.

HARRY Shinning?

MAUDIE Just my hands and knees. And because gran and grandad would be out, at every change of programme since the telly broke, I'd go out and climb the lamp-post. And the other children would pull back to watch. (HARRY *chuckles, identifying with the experience*) Sometimes I'd climb even higher than the light. I would catch the iron thing on top and pull myself up over the top, and sit there in the night. And sometimes, if I waited up there long enough, everything made— sense.

HARRY (*A little jealous of this last experience*) Did you ever hear of Ivan the Terrible?

MAUDIE (*Nods, but she is not listening to him*) It were very exciting.

HARRY That was my name when I topped the bill.

MAUDIE (*Nods*) And then I'd come sliding down and the others cheering, 'Maudie—Maudie—Maudie!' That's what they always said, 'Maudie — Maudie — Maudie!'

Except—it were funny—when two of the older boys that sometimes come along, and they always said 'Maud, Maud!'

HARRY   Pass that ball of paper—Maud. (*They laugh. She hands him the paper that wrapped the bread*)

MAUDIE   'Who taught you how to climb poles, Maud?' And I'd say 'Jesus!' (*They laugh*) And sometimes I'd come sliding down and then I'd do cartwheels. Do you know cartwheels?

HARRY   Oh, indeed.

MAUDIE   Or stand on my head? (*He nods*) Or there were another. I'd come sliding down, I wouldn't have stopped, but keep on running into our house, and I'd open the window, and I'd have stood on the table, and I'd've took off my clothes, and stick my bottom out at them. And they'd be cheering 'Maudie—Maudie—Maudie!' And the two bigger boys ——

HARRY   Maud! Maud!

MAUDIE   Yes. 'Maud, Maud, come out a minute'. Sort of whispering.

HARRY   And would you? . . . go out again?

        MAUDIE *is now looking gravely at him. She nods. Now she is near tears.*

MAUDIE   Shall I tell you?

HARRY   No ——

MAUDIE   Shall I not tell you?

HARRY   No, that was quite successful ——

MAUDIE   (*Crying*) But it's started up again ——

HARRY   Another topic—what shall we talk about?

MAUDIE   Not dreaming—not dreaming! ——

HARRY   (*Trying to think of something to offer her*) I know: would you like— would you like ——

MAUDIE   I just want it to stop ——

HARRY   Maudie, would you like ——

MAUDIE   Forgiveness. Forgiveness.

HARRY   Maudie, Maudie.

MAUDIE   (*Dismally*) Shall I not tell you?

HARRY   Old favourite actually. (*Sings*) 'When the red red robin goes bob-bob-bobbin' along. When the red red robin goes bob-bob-bobbin' along. Get up, giddy up' —Maudie.

MAUDIE   What?

HARRY   (*Indicates a pillar, jocosely inviting her to climb it*)
           Would you? ——

MAUDIE   What? (*Then laughing, drying her tears*) It's too fat.

HARRY   Do you know any songs? Hmm? And then I might
           go out and buy some— Well, let's see how we get on.
           Do you know any songs?

MAUDIE   (*Sings*) 'Put your head upon my pillow; hold your
           warm and tender body close to mine; hear the whistle
           of the raindrops blowing up against my window; and
           make believe you love me one more time; for the
           good times, for the good times, for the good times.'

HARRY   That was very nice. Hmm?

MAUDIE   Tired.

HARRY   Yes. It's important that you get your sleep. Where
           do you sleep?

MAUDIE   In one of those boxes. (*The confessionals*)

HARRY   In the vertical? Too ventilated in the vertical, and bad
           for the circulation. We can be getting it ready. (*He
           starts to remove the brooms etc. from the confessional*)
           The horizontal gives better protection against the
           breezes. So, we'll lay it on the floor. I think we're
           safe now against the Monsignor showing up.

MAUDIE   And there are plenty of cushions and things about.

HARRY   Yes, start collecting a few of them (*She goes*) but
           remember where you took them from! We can get in
           a little store of tea, sugar, brown bread and butter
           tomorrow. And jam. Actually, the most thing we
           need—it crossed my mind today—a little extractor fan
           for in there. (*The sacristy*) With a little extractor fan
           no odours of cooking about in the morning. Would
           you like a drink of water? (*She nods*) Follow me.

           *She follows him to the threshold of sacristy and
           stands there. He exits for a cup of water.*

MAUDIE   Is he (*Jesus*) awake?

HARRY   (*Off*) Oh yes.

           *She considers the sanctuary lamp silently for a
           moment.*

           (*Returning*) And starting tomorrow we'll buy some
           utensils. (*He gives her the water*) We'll buy a pan—if
           the Monsignor thinks to sub me. And when we get

25

our pan, cook some nice calf's liver, and onions. And if he doesn't think to give me the subbies, we'll have to tap St. Anthony—(*He chuckles*) for the short term. Enough?

MAUDIE Ta. (*She hands him the cup.* HARRY *exits with the cup*) Does he sit on a throne?

HARRY (*Off*) Do you see a throne? (*Returning*) Well then. No, more like a wheel-chair, if he's sitting on anything, but we'll soon take care of that. And a little bit of decoration around here would do no harm. (*The clock starts to chime twelve*) Yes, I think we're safe now. (*He catches the top of the confessional. He pauses for a moment*) If we could think of the proper place to put the fan.

MAUDIE We could stay here forever!

HARRY (*Lowering the confessional to a horizontal position on the floor*) Hup! Hup! Voilà! (*They laugh at their confessional-bed. They are delighted with themselves.* HARRY—*the circus strongman—skips back from the confessional*) Ivan the Terrible! Voilà! Voilà! (*He considers the pulpit momentarily: rejects idea. He strikes poses*) Here, Maudie! What am I doing? Holding back six horses! Here, Maudie! You be my assistant. Like this: watch! (*He demonstrates the movements he wishes her to perform. She obliges*) Then say 'Voilà!' 'Voilà!' Means, 'See!' 'Behold', actually, that's what it means. (*He is lying on his back on the floor*) What am I doing? A plank across my arms and chest, lifting four, six, eight, ten tall men!

MAUDIE Voilà!

HARRY Hup! (*He is on his feet again: considering the pulpit*)

MAUDIE You nearly lifted it. I was watching.

He is going to the pulpit, then changes his mind, smiles to himself. Now his movements balletic, reminiscent of a child dancing.

HARRY No. Everything is alright now. I'll look after you, Maudie.

MAUDIE (*Reacting to something off*) Shh!

HARRY It was no simple stroke of luck that led me here. (*They are reacting to a noise outside. He takes out his knife*) Francisco! (*Listens again*) The governor's here! Hurry, quick, cave!

26

He sends her down the church in one direction, he grabs an armful of the cushions—there isn't time to replace the confessional—and hurries off in another direction. During this the MONSIGNOR *is heard unlocking the sacristy door.* MONSIGNOR *enters. He stands looking at the comparative disarray, confessional lying on the floor, etc.*

MONSIGNOR Harry! . . . Harry! . . . Anybody here?

FRANCISCO has entered the church, secretly following MONSIGNOR, *and hides.* MONSIGNOR *begins to move in the direction that* MAUDIE *has taken.* HARRY *enters.*

HARRY Ah—Monsignor—Excuse. But I waited on to do a few chores . . . That old confessional: I thought I'd give it a good scrub out tomorrow. If walls could talk!

MONSIGNOR Yes. I'm sorry. I had meant to be back to lock up with you but I got caught up in . . . (*The book*)

HARRY Actually, I thought you might, so—y'know? (HARRY *picks up the paper that wrapped the bread, holds it out so that* MONSIGNOR *can see it is a thing of nothing and puts it in his pocket*)

MONSIGNOR So . . . I think everything is in order.

HARRY Excuse for just a . . .

HARRY *lifts the confessional, returning it to its proper position.* MONSIGNOR *watches him and sighs, now understanding better* HARRY'S *state and circumstances.*

MONSIGNOR Thank you, Harry.

HARRY Monsignor.

MONSIGNOR So I think everything is in order. (*He is reluctant to leave: wondering what can he do for* HARRY) Yes, I got caught up in the book. Finished it.

HARRY Good?

MONSIGNOR Yes. Yes, it was, actually. (*The awareness of the futility of his day's achievement in his smile*) So . . . (*He makes a move as if to leave*)

HARRY Ah—Excuse—But— (*He indicates the replacement candle which* MONSIGNOR *has picked up*)

27

MONSIGNOR Oh. That's alright. (*He leaves the candle somewhere.* HARRY *momentarily concerned for the lamp*) Were you happy in the circus?

HARRY Oh yes. Well, early on. Before I—y'know? Actually, in my category, I was rated one of the four strongest men in the world.

MONSIGNOR Were you?

HARRY Y'know?

MONSIGNOR Yes.

HARRY Sixteen stone weight above my head before I was sixteen.

MONSIGNOR Yes, I saw you were a cut above the average.

HARRY But I don't mind admitting I'm very happy here.

MONSIGNOR Yes.

Pause.

MONSIGNOR ⎱ Is there anything I can ——
HARRY   ⎰ Is the ——

MONSIGNOR Yes?

HARRY Is the Pope infallible?

MONSIGNOR Well, the last one was, the next one will be, but we're not so sure about the present fella. Anything I can do for you, Harry? . . . Things go wrong for people, don't they? All of us need help one way or another . . . In my own case, I'm not sure what went wrong. Was led to expect a certain position some years ago, and when the seat—position—became vacant, I was passed over in a regular piece of church jiggery-pokery, and fobbed off with one of the new semi-detacheds—detacheds—that were built with the new school. What? . . . No, of course I had no right to allow myself to be led to expect anything, had I? No, the real reason: lost my humility. If I ever had any. Humility, what? A cunning way of dealing with God. Yes. Well, point is . . . what is the point? (*He laughs to himself*) That wasn't much help, was it? What I'm saying is, I'm not a totally lost soul and I've never turned anybody away from that same semi-detached. Detached. Extraordinary word. (*To enunciate*) I can offer people shelter. What do you say?

HARRY I've a very good head for heights actually, and I know where you can hire extremely excellent scaffolding— mobile kind, on castors, y'know?, and I wouldn't

         ⎱ mind having a go at painting that ceiling.
MONSIGNOR ⎰ Hum, hum, haa!
    HARRY   Only cost you the price of the paint.
MONSIGNOR ⎰ No, what I'm saying is ——
   HARRY ⎱ No charge for the labour of course.
MONSIGNOR People stay at my place from time to time ——
    HARRY Goes without saying, labour would be gratis ——
MONSIGNOR Until they get fixed up. Plenty of books there, that sort of thing.
    HARRY But do you not see the roof is falling in! (*Then by way of apology for his sharpness he adds*) Y'know?
MONSIGNOR Yes. Shall we? (*Go*) (*He is going to switch off the lights: stops*) But, just for your information, Harry, before coming here I called to the Paxton Street address to see if you'd managed okay. Chap there, cheeky chappie, had some drink taken I think. Said you didn't live there anymore. I thought I'd tell you: he seemed—eager—to find you. I didn't tell him where you were.
    HARRY (*Muted*) Monsignor.
MONSIGNOR You're more than welcome to stay at my place until you get things straightened out.
    HARRY (*Firmly, to himself*) I'm going to get things straightened out. May I—y'know? (*Go*)
    HARRY Tut-tut, of no account. May I? (*Go*)
MONSIGNOR Why don't you call and see me at ten, or eleven—Whatever time suits you best.
    HARRY Monsignor.

> *And exits purposefully.* MONSIGNOR *switches off the lights and exits a moment later.* MAUDIE *appears cautiously: she stands there looking after them.* FRANCISCO *appearing from behind a pillar.* MAUDIE *retreating to the shadows,* FRANCISCO *following her: he stops, whispers*

FRANCISCO Excuse me! . . . Excuse me!

> *Music up, lights down.*

Half an hour later. MAUDIE *and* FRANCISCO *in the church.* FRANCISCO *is drinking a bottle of altar wine. He is in his thirties, Irish, self-destructive, usually considered a blackguard, but there are reasons for his behaviour. Greasy hair, an earring, and the faded flash of zip-jacket over dirty slacks and plimsolls. Unshaven.*

FRANCISCO ... Know what I mean? (MAUDIE'S *face is blank*) Alright. Can God do anything? ... Well, say he can, right? Right. Well can he make a stone he cannot lift? ... Okay. You believe in God, right? (MAUDIE *considers it. Then nods*) Right. God made the world, right?, and fair play to him. What has he done since? Tell me. Right, I'll tell you. Evaporated himself. When they painted his toe-nails and turned him into a church he lost his ambition, gave up learning, stagnated for a while, then gave up even that, said fuck it, forget it, and became a vague pain in his own and everybody else's arse. (MAUDIE *laughs at the four letter words*) Aha, you see! We know each other alright. (*He offers her a drink: she declines*) Take Jesus. Jesus was A-one. Know what I mean? But they've nearly written him out of existence. He might as well have been Napoleon. As a matter of fact I think that all concerned would have been better off. Supposing the Holy Ghost, or whosoever, had chosen to do a few tricks with old Napoleon Bonaparte, this whole cosmos would be a different kettle of fish. (*Offers drink again: she declines*) Sure, Maud? I don't think he's (HARRY) coming back. No, as a fairly experienced punter, in the three horse race of the Trinity, I'm inclined to give my vote to your man, the Holy Spirit. Alias the Friendly Ghost. He's the coming man. Would you agree? But, yes, yes, maybe you're right, because—yes, yes—when you think of it, him being symbolised by a dove and all that, I'm inclined to agree that he was the original bat in the belfry. What? So how are you going to get forgiveness from that lot? Have you ever thought who's going to forgive them? Who's going to forgive the Gods? Hmm?

(*Laughs*) So the state they must be in! What? There's no such thing as forgiveness.

MAUDIE There is.

FRANCISCO There isn't.

MAUDIE There is.

FRANCISCO Hmm? . . . And is Harry looking for forgiveness too? (MAUDIE *shrugs*) He should be.

MAUDIE Strength, I think.

FRANCISCO And I'd like the whole place to fall down. (*In reaction to a smile from her*) What?

MAUDIE Not with yourself inside.

FRANCISCO And singing and dancing and talking to Jesus here and everything? Very nice.

MAUDIE Not *really* dancing.

FRANCISCO Not really dancing? Still, very nice. And he's looking for strength? What has he been saying about me? . . . Did he mention what great friends we were? (MAUDIE *shrugs*) Did he tell you I'm his best friend?

MAUDIE No.

FRANCISCO Oh yes, Old Har and I are the last of the Texas Rangers. (*To himself*) And I have some news for my friend.

The clock chimes one o'clock.

There: one o'clock. I really don't think he's coming back. What?

MAUDIE I think he might have gone to buy some fish and chips.

FRANCISCO No, I'm telling you, he got the push from the coonic. So why not come back to my place in Paxton Street? There's no one else there now. Maud? . . . Well, I'll tell you, we'll give him another five minutes, okay? Then we'll blow . . . Cold, isn't it? I find it very hard to be on my own. Find it very hard to sleep on my own. Do you? (*He has his arm around her*)

MAUDIE What are you doing?

FRANCISCO Just take my hand then.

MAUDIE (*Considers it, then*) No.

FRANCISCO Okay. (*He lights a cigarette*)—Oh, do you want one?

MAUDIE (*Considers it, then*) No.

FRANCISCO I can't sleep sometimes because I can't stop thinking. Know what I mean?

MAUDIE I'm always thinking.

FRANCISCO Yeh? Do you do the trick for him?

MAUDIE   What?

FRANCISCO   Okay. What do you think about?

MAUDIE   . . . Everything.

FRANCISCO   Yeh? I think about all the flesh in the world. And all the hopes. *And* the prayers. And all the passions of the passions, in heaps higher than all the cathedrals, burning in a constant flame. And my own heart, the fuse, keeping things burning. And if it blows, so does the lot. That's what I think about. What do you think about? And I'd love to stop thinking.

MAUDIE   So would I.

FRANCISCO   Yeh? (*She nods*)

MAUDIE   I think about Stephen.

FRANCISCO   Stephen? Another boyfriend?

MAUDIE   A boyfriend?—Stephen! No! Not a boyfriend.

FRANCISCO   Yeh? (*She averts her eyes*) . . . You have a baby, Maud? Stephen? Is that who you think about? At night? Awake and asleep?

MAUDIE   What?

FRANCISCO   Did he die? Did you have him adopted?

MAUDIE   . . . Shall I tell you?

FRANCISCO   Take my hand. Yeh?

MAUDIE   Do you know—hospitals? Well, my grandad said let someone else take care of me. Well, I come home late one night and he were waiting. In the hall. In his bare feet. And he found eight new p. in my pocket. *I* don't know how it got there. Maybe one of the bigger boys. And grandad said he would have kicked me, if he had his boots on. And grandad said let someone else take care of me to have a baby. And gran was lucky to find me one of those hospitals. And I had a baby. I knew he were not well. But I knew if I could not take care of him, who could? And once I woke and they were taking him away. And I growled. But there were an old— Do you know nuns? Well, there were an old nun. She were in black, the others were in white, and she were my friend. And she said had I thought of a name for him. *I* hadn't thought of a name. And she said would I call him Stephen. Because that were her name. And she would like that. And I said okay. And they smiled—the way I said 'okay'. And I laughed. But I were not happy at all. But I were so warm and sleepy. But I wanted to sit up so they'd see I were not happy. Because I were crying. So they took him away to baptize him. Because he were not well. And the next time I woke up, only the old nun were there. And she come to me, sort of smiling and frowning together. And she said 'Maudie. Maudie'. like that. Like as if I were asleep. But I were awake. I were wide awake. And she said, 'Stephen is dead, Maudie. Stephen is with Jesus'. At first I didn't know if she were only fibbing, but when he started to visit me—No, not dreaming! Not dreaming! So all around me—I knew he were dead alright. But I didn't tell them. Because I wanted them to let me go. And I didn't want the other patients to pull my hair. I only told the old nun. To ask her would it stop. And she said it would, in time. And I said, when I get forgiveness, was it? And she said yes.

FRANCISCO *feels commiseration but he reacts harshly.*

FRANCISCO There's no such thing! (MAUDIE *is near tears. She looks at him*) No such thing. That's not thinking—that's dreaming.
MAUDIE What? . . . That's what gran said about my mam.
FRANCISCO Dreaming.
MAUDIE Then why doesn't it stop?
FRANCISCO I don't know. Dreaming!
MAUDIE Is it? . . . And with fair hair and blue eyes.
FRANCISCO What colour are your eyes?
MAUDIE Brown.
FRANCISCO That's it: dreaming.
MAUDIE Well I just want him to stop. To say he's alright and to stop.

FRANCISCO *sighs. Pause.*

FRANCISCO Night is a funny time, isn't it?
MAUDIE Is that what you think? (*He nods*)
FRANCISCO . . . (*Gently*) That's dreaming, Maud. (*She looks at him*) Quite frankly it must be, or else you're daft. (*He smiles. Then she smiles. He laughs, then she laughs*) When I was young, really young, do you know what I used to think about every night?—What age are you?
MAUDIE *My* age?

FRANCISCO   You're over sixteen, aren't you?

MAUDIE   I was sixteen on the 21st February.

FRANCISCO   And what do you do?

MAUDIE   What do *I* do?

FRANCISCO   Yeh. Job.

MAUDIE   Me?

FRANCISCO   Yeh.

MAUDIE   *I* don't have a job.

FRANCISCO   And you won't come back to Paxton Street with me? . . . Hmm?

MAUDIE   Did you think I had a job.

FRANCISCO   Yeh. Call me Francisco, Maud. Know what I mean?

MAUDIE   Alright.

> *They hear* HARRY *returning.* FRANCISCO *looks frightened, stubs out his cigarette, then puts a finger to his lips warning* MAUDIE *to keep silent.* FRANCISCO *hides.* MAUDIE *hiding a giggle at this game.* HARRY *enters by side door (the key he stole earlier). He has a small parcel. Then* FRANCISCO *is heard singing.* HARRY'S *hand to his pocket for his knife, then decides to play it coolly.*

FRANCISCO   'God of mercy and compassion, look with pity upon me; Father, let me call thee Father, 'tis thy child returns to thee—' (*He comes out of hiding*) 'Jesus Lord, I ask for mercy, let me not implore in vain—' Harry! (*Laughs*) Jesus Lord! Jesus Lord! (*Sings*) 'All my sins I now detest them; never will I sin again'. Harry! For what reason have I this fortnight been a banished pal from my friend Harry?

HARRY   Oh, hello, Francisco. That was very—y'know? (*The singing*) (*He glances at the bottle of wine*)

FRANCISCO   I took the liberty of helping myself. They owe it to me.

HARRY   Not at all, old boy. I knew you'd show up.

FRANCISCO   What's with the running out on us like that?

HARRY   You're looking very well.

FRANCISCO   What's with the giving me the run around, Hymie? (HARRY *pauses for a moment, then walks past* FRANCISCO *returning to the side door*) Won't you join me? (*In a drink*)

HARRY   (*Exiting*) Not at the moment, old boy. (*We hear* HARRY *off, locking the door*)

FRANCISCO What's he doing?
MAUDIE Locking the door.

HARRY *returns, affecting to ignore* FRANCISCO.

FRANCISCO Won't you join me? (*Offering wine*)
HARRY No thank you. (*He produces fish and chips from his parcel*)
FRANCISCO Won't she? (*Have a drink*) Maud?
HARRY Quite in order, Maudie—if you wish. Would you like a . . . Get a cup. (*As* MAUDIE *exits to the sacristy*)
FRANCISCO Get two cups . . . She's a big young girl, Har?
HARRY Oh yes.
FRANCISCO (*A dirty laugh*) Hah?
HARRY Indeed.
FRANCISCO Well, it's good to see you, fella!
HARRY You're looking very well, extremely so, how are you?
FRANCISCO Terrific. Here comes Maud.
HARRY I was actually on my way to visit you outside just now but, there you are, I turned back.

MAUDIE *has returned with two cups.* HARRY *pours a cup of wine for her.*

FRANCISCO Have some, Har.
HARRY No thank you, old boy.

HARRY *has taken out his penknife and divides the fish between himself and* MAUDIE, *excluding* FRANCISCO. *Though feigning casualness and affecting to ignore* FRANCISCO, *his movements are tense and deliberate.*

I took the liberty, Maudie, of getting some fish and chips. Not enough money for two pieces and they were actually sold out of cod. But never mind, haddock's very nice too.
MAUDIE Ta.
FRANCISCO Not gefülte fish!
HARRY Very nice, mind you. Just, it hasn't got the same beneficial juices.
FRANCISCO I was educated—brought up you could say—by the Jesuits. Give me a child until he is seven they say, and then you can have him back! If there's one thing

35

my life disproves it's that. And that's what I aim to go on disproving.

HARRY (*To* MAUDIE *who he feels is giving too much attention to* FRANCISCO) Not too much vinegar I hope, Maudie?

MAUDIE (*Shakes her head, then to* FRANCISCO) Does Jesus give back the child?

FRANCISCO Jesuits, Jesuits.

HARRY (*To* MAUDIE) Hmm?

MAUDIE What's a Jesuit?

FRANCISCO It is a distortion of a Jesus with sex in the head and tendencies towards violence! (*He laughs*) I have a dream! I have a dream! The day is coming, the not too distant future! The housewives of the capitals of the world—Yea, the housewives of the very Vatican itself, marching daily to the altar-rails to be administered of the pill at the hands of the priest himself!

HARRY Yours alright, Maudie? (*She nods but is inclined to laugh with* FRANCISCO)

FRANCISCO Here's one. What's a curate trying to be a parish priest? A mouse trying to be a rat!

HARRY Not too much salt I hope, Maudie? (*She shakes her head*)

FRANCISCO We had this great chat, Har, Maud and me, and she told me all. And I was telling her what great friends we were. Do you know what he did one night? The drinking and carousing in the old days! We came out of this pub, and suddenly, there's Harry with his false teeth in his hand, throws them on the ground and starts dancing on them. 'I'll have nothing false in my head.' Har, remember?

HARRY (*To* MAUDIE) Not too much— too much— y'know?

MAUDIE No.

FRANCISCO What's all the cold shoulder for? Do you sleep with women, my son? I doze, father, I doze!

HARRY (*Reacts angrily for a moment*) Just a moment, old boy! We're— y'know— dining. (*Pause.* HARRY *and* MAUDIE *continue eating*)

FRANCISCO (*Quietly*) Take me to that millionaire in Rome and I'll walk theologically all over him. (*He sits with his arm around* MAUDIE) Maud and I were nearly going off when you were out. Weren't we? (MAUDIE *giggles*)

HARRY What? (*Sharply to* MAUDIE) And certain things are very naughty— very wicked things to be doing! So, y'know?— Eat up, and then the waste, refuse, to be

FRANCISCO disposed of. Et cetera.

FRANCISCO What are you talking about?

HARRY Just a second, old boy. Not too glib now. Remember that movie queen, Maria Del Nostro? I had her.

FRANCISCO What?

HARRY I'd just like you all to know that. The ladies always came after me. For sex, actually. Very enjoyable. Y'know? Which is more than can be said for— (FRANCISCO) and— (OLGA) Film stars. Very charming. Remember the Irish-American prima donna actually, Chastity O'Casey. (*He nods, meaning he had her too*) Sixteen years of age. (HARRY *was sixteen*) My first time.

FRANCISCO What's with the confession?

HARRY Took her over the sticks. A hunting lodge, Maudie. And I was up at three, half three and a quarter to four, waiting for tomorrow, waiting for the dawn to go hunting. And whom should I see arriving at the lodge with a member of our party but the goddess—she was goddess actually—Chastity O'Casey. I ran back to my bed, heard them clumping up the stairs, and the member of our party going into the— y'know?— where it was obvious he was being sick. And where a few minutes later he had obviously actually collapsed. Then some moments later my door flew open and in strode the Irish-American prima donna, Chastity O'Casey, and said 'Hey, son, you're doing nothing there, come on'. So, y'see?

FRANCISCO I remember Chastity O'Casey. Vaguely.

HARRY They always came looking for me, Maudie. I never had to be sneaky.

FRANCISCO Who am I sneaking now?

HARRY Also you're a very bad juggler.

FRANCISCO Chastity O'Casey: must be dead twenty years now. Some tribes have these rites of initiation: like scourging, tatooing, or knocking out their front teeth. Harry had Chastity O'Casey.

HARRY Just like you all to know that. I'm not one to brag normally, and I would like to apologise for mentioning the ladies' names in question.

FRANCISCO I was talking about ——

HARRY Just a second, old boy! More wine, Maudie?

FRANCISCO Later days.

HARRY Later days?

FRANCISCO When we met. We must have been the first pair of Bohemians around these parts. The laughs we had, Har. He had started to go downhill— (HARRY *glances at him*) slightly. I mean I hadn't even started uphill. Remember the little yellow plastic bucket, Har?

HARRY No.

FRANCISCO We had this little yellow plastic bucket, Maud, and we had a bicycle. Me on the carrier with the bucket, and Harry peddling, up and down the road the two of us, always laughing, we'd wash a few cars and we had enough to get by until tomorrow.

HARRY Don't remember.

FRANCISCO But, of course, that had to end. My best friend deserted me. Got married, middle-class values, the lot, a little woman.

HARRY Middle-class values: going back to the circus?

FRANCISCO Respectability, new shoes ——

HARRY Took you in again ——

FRANCISCO You sent for me!

HARRY Took you in again, got you a job.

FRANCISCO But I think it was the new shoes that got me most of all.

HARRY Took you in, got the sack, lost the lot.

FRANCISCO Ah, they were not long, those plastic bucket days of wine and roses! (HARRY *stands suddenly*)

HARRY What do you want?

FRANCISCO What?

HARRY I'm not a fool, Francisco! What are all these— memories—about?

FRANCISCO . . . I just dropped in: for God's sake. (*Then soberly, quietly*) We could start again. You'll be looking for something new now anyway.

HARRY Something new?

FRANCISCO I heard the coonic talking to you.

HARRY A Monsignor actually. Very decent, very charming.

FRANCISCO I was listening.

HARRY I'd like to see someone raise a finger to him.

FRANCISCO Giving you the sack.

HARRY Cheekie chappie, he said.

FRANCISCO Giving you the bullet.

HARRY I thought you might follow him— I knew you'd show up.

FRANCISCO He fired you!

HARRY Oh no.

FRANCISCO I heard him!

HARRY Got it wrong.

FRANCISCO (*Appeals to her*) Maud!

HARRY It doesn't change things!

FRANCISCO It doesn't . . .?

HARRY We'll still go on living here!

FRANCISCO Be realistic!

HARRY It's all worked out!—We'll still go on— And you will keep the little secret of our residence— Be realistic?— won't you? (FRANCISCO *is now more conscious of the threat and of the penknife in* HARRY'S *hand*)

FRANCISCO Okay. (*Moving a little away from* HARRY: *he picks up the wine bottle and demonstrates that it is empty. To* MAUDIE) This altar wine has gone to my head.

HARRY Put it down. (*The bottle*)

FRANCISCO (*Still talking to* MAUDIE) I'm more accustomed to the humbler 'table' wine.

HARRY Francisco!

FRANCISCO You from round here, Maud?

HARRY Tell him to mind his own ——

MAUDIE (*To* FRANCISCO) I'm from 32 Rock's Lane. (HARRY *is growing confused by* FRANCISCO'S *attitude and by his feeling of* MAUDIE'S *shifting allegiance*)

HARRY Francisco!—(*Turns to* MAUDIE) Waste—refuse—Dispose of! (*To* FRANCISCO) Put it down.

FRANCISCO (*Puts down the bottle*) Okay. Okay, forget it. (*He is moving away*)

HARRY Where do you think you're going?

FRANCISCO (*Stops*) Another bottle of bourgeois.

HARRY Just a moment. (HARRY *goes to* FRANCISCO *and sends him sprawling with a punch*) Now can we be civil?

FRANCISCO Aw, for fuck's sake! What's the matter with you? (HARRY *is coming for him again*) I've something to tell you! (HARRY *hits him again, flattening him this time*)

HARRY See him! See him! See him, Maudie! So I'm not as— y'know?—dilapidated as you might think. Now, why do you give everyone in the world a hard time?

FRANCISCO Well, this is one for the book.

HARRY What?

FRANCISCO A half-lapsed Jew here ——

HARRY Francisco!

FRANCISCO In residence ——

HARRY Francisco!

FRANCISCO A Catholic church, with a young chick.

HARRY   Or I shall have to make the other ear pop. See him! Not so cocky as he was. Not so cocky as when last I saw you. Yes, get another bottle of wine, Maudie. (*She does not move*) Get it! (*She goes*) Do Olga and Sam know I'm here? . . . Do you hear me, Francisco?

FRANCISCO I don't know.

HARRY   What?

FRANCISCO No. God only knows how many sacrileges you've committed here!

HARRY   Oh no.

FRANCISCO Yes!

HARRY   You believe in nothing, so, as far as you're concerned I've committed nothing, see? (MAUDIE *returns with a bottle of wine which* HARRY *uncorks, etc.*) See him? You have nothing, Francisco. You, Olga, or Sam. I always believed in things. And when you have nothing and you believe in nothing, you have nothing at all!

FRANCISCO Oh, I have a few things.

HARRY   Like what, for instance?

FRANCISCO (*His face expressing his loathing and impotence*) Oh, I have a few things.

HARRY   Like my wife for instance? How is she? Hmm? Do— you—hear—me!

FRANCISCO Fine. (HARRY *chuckles*)

HARRY   And those little plastic bucket days: just a few years for me, interim actually. (*He takes a slug from the new bottle of wine, then places it near* FRANCISCO) Your wine, Francisco. Something to tell me? (FRANCISCO *takes a drink. Through the following his attitude swings from artifice to abandon*)

FRANCISCO (*Mutters*) I've something to tell you alright.

HARRY   What did you say?

FRANCISCO Unless you resolve to suffer and die things will not get better says the Lord! Speak up, speak up, Lord, your servant is listening! So, you've found yourself here, Har, have you? You find yourself here too, Maud? And I lost myself in a place like this.

HARRY   Have you something to tell me?

FRANCISCO Yeh? Can I top up yours, Maud? Can I top up hers, Har? (*He laughs harshly*)

HARRY   Francisco!

FRANCISCO (*Harshly*) Yes, Har! What I was looking for you for, was to tell you how that last engagement went. The one you walked out on. The biggest engagement we ever got and he disappeared. Sidon, blush for shame, says the sea!

HARRY Yes?

FRANCISCO You're interested, are you?

HARRY Must confess: trifle curious.

FRANCISCO Yeh? Well, hang on. Cheers! (*He drinks again*) Well that final gig. *And* its consequences.

HARRY Did you not get another engagement since then? (HARRY *is pleased*)

FRANCISCO Yeh? Yes, I can see that you're happy here in the bosom of blind old Abraham. But that last engagement. No doubt it was an experience not to be missed. And—*and*—they didn't ask old Olga to do a strip: I bet that will surprise you. Does that not surprise you? Har?

HARRY (*Uncomfortable*) Oh yes?

FRANCISCO Oh, sorry—sorry!—sorry for talking shop, love. Has he not told you about our line of business? Have you not told her about—? Hmm?

HARRY No.

FRANCISCO What! Did you not see our ad in *The Times*? 'All the thrills of the circus, live in your drawingroom'. And whose idea do you think it was? (*Points at* HARRY) The very man. The celebrity. (HARRY *makes some move, looking dangerous*) Well, we all contributed. So maybe we are all to blame.

HARRY Blame?

FRANCISCO So long as we could perform.

HARRY What blame?

FRANCISCO The showman must go on. Right Har? This senseless desire that *some* of us had to please. And be liked.

HARRY What are you on about?

FRANCISCO We were on a good thing. Not many engagements but forty nicker a time when we got them. And for that last engagement, well, with just three of us, we demanded only thirty.

HARRY Francisco ——

FRANCISCO I just want to explain to Maud, and to Jesus there. Cause she told me all. But the perks were always good. Weren't they, Har? Har?

HARRY Oh yes.

FRANCISCO We got the grub. Free gargle. Why, the most VSOP ten-year-old Napoleon Bonapartes for him always.

And we'd nick some grub, nick some sauce. And you know this two-and-a-half foot friend of ours, Maud? Do you know the first thing little Sam would do on a Saturday night engagement? Check the hostess's fridge for our Sunday joint! Oh, a very carnally-minded little man was Sam. Right, Har? (HARRY *cautious, vigilant, but amused*) And do you know how he'd get it out? Smuggle it out, by using it as a hump!

HARRY   Aw, Francisco! ——

FRANCISCO   And needless to say, no one ever searches a dwarf.

HARRY   Don't you believe him. (*He chuckles*)

FRANCISCO   Clever?

HARRY   Aw, Francisco.

FRANCISCO   (*Smiling humourlessly*) What, Har? (HARRY *remembering that the situation is not funny; his penknife held aloft to remind* FRANCISCO *that he has got him where he wants him.* FRANCISCO *nods*) But to return to Olga, Olga, Olga. Well, why not, in answer to the calls of a world in search of sensation shouldn't a good-natured husband and a philosophical best man allow her to strip? Y'know—y'know—y'know! What, Har?—Sorry, Har?—I didn't hear, Har? And, Maud, post-striptease at our engagements, the host was always allowed to chat old Olga up, for the slice. Know what I mean? And, or, optionally, alternatively, one or two other selected guests. This senseless desire we had to please. You see? And be liked. (HARRY's *head is bowed.* FRANCISCO *is watching him*) Oh we were a band intimate! (FRANCISCO *tip-toes away and hides in the pulpit.* HARRY *becomes aware of the silence and looks about for* FRANCISCO)

HARRY   Francisco!

FRANCISCO   (*Shows himself in the pulpit*) Don't let your soul suffer from neglect!

HARRY   Come down!

FRANCISCO   But the pattern of man's sins will be the pattern of his punishment. See the depraved ones, who so loved their own pleasures, now bathing in black, hot, bubbling pitch and reeking sulphur! See the gluttonous pigs, now parched and hungry!

HARRY   Come down!

FRANCISCO   And what of the tardy-footed giants who did not lift a finger? See them: masters of sorrow, go howling like dogs for very grief! Do you want absolution, Har?

HARRY　Come down!

> HARRY *is coming towards* FRANCISCO. *FRANCISCO pulls up the little ladder which leads to the pulpit.*

FRANCISCO　Know what I mean, Har? The ones who didn't lift a finger—but who now claim they know better. (HARRY *starts to lurch at the pulpit and* FRANCISCO *produces a candlestick which he can obviously use as a weapon*) Y'know—y'know—y'know! There was no one but myself to kiss away the tears of that poor, unhappy, lost, unfaithful wife.

HARRY　And Teresa?

FRANCISCO　Yes.

HARRY　And Teresa!

FRANCISCO　Everyone to blame but you, Har? (HARRY *rushes in, and with a mighty effort lifts the pulpit off its base*) Hup! Hup! Voilà!

HARRY　See! See!

> HARRY *lets the pulpit down. He is panting, doubled up, after his effort but is proud of his achievement.*

FRANCISCO　Bravo!

HARRY　See! See! Come down now, Francisco.

FRANCISCO　Something to tell you, Har. Y'know—y'know—y'know!

HARRY　Alright, I can wait.

FRANCISCO　I haven't told you about that last engagement yet.

HARRY　(*To* MAUDIE) See?

FRANCISCO　*And* its consequences.

> *In the foregoing and in the following there is a strange import in* FRANCISCO'S *references to* OLGA, *which makes* HARRY *pause—but only fleetingly:* HARRY *keeps banishing the thought that* OLGA, *too, is dead. The clock chimes the half hour.* FRANCISCO *goes through the motions of checking the time on an imaginary pocket watch and placing it in front of him.*

FRANCISCO　My dear brethren in Christ, the story of the critic's ball. Or, is there not always a kind of melancholy attaching to the glory we attain in this world? Some of you are no doubt aware of a certain troupe who were called upon one evening to tender service, and sow the seeds of merriment at the mansion of a mighty man who writes only for the most important papers and who even has his own television show. Why, it was said of this man that he could turn an artist into a cult. Didn't we say that, Har?

HARRY Not a dirty story now, Francisco.

FRANCISCO No—no—no. Anyways, as Harry says, we got to the place ——

HARRY Really got you where I want you now, Francisco.

FRANCISCO (*Nods, agreeing*) There were two large rooms adjoining for the party. One for the intellectuals, drink-sipping and telling dirty stories, the other for drink-slopping, dancing, and groping, which I think they call goosing. There were people there from all nations. The mandatory one black was there of course, T.V. personalities, people from the press, jilly-journalists—Don't be talking!—talking about appliances, perversions, performances, their faces sexually awake as current buns. And so on. It was our big break. Well, we performed and, truth to tell, I think it was not of our best. (HARRY *chuckles*) Yes, I'll admit that. Howandever, Har, I'm glad to say that when we were through, the intellectuals would have nothing but our joining them in their very own room. And you know how nobody ever touches a dwarf? Well, I'm glad to say that as we stood 'round in an obedient circle, our champagne glasses to attention, Sam stood proudly at the great man's leg, the great man's fingers, stiff as pencils, gently resting on Sam's shoulder. Oh, the great man knew your name, Har, and of your erstwhile fame, and many were the regrets expressed at your inability to be among us.

HARRY Oh yes?

FRANCISCO But we were enjoying ourselves. And why not? And everyone was secretly congratulating himself on fitting in so well in such manifest civilization. And one wondered what could possibly go wrong. Well, in the most civilized of manners, Olga, not in our circle, but following the usual pattern that we'd all agreed upon, was smiling 'cross the crowded room at our host and employer. Whose expression betrayed the double-meaning that he would not have minded the slice at all, but that he found something in old Olga a trifle frightening. So, the seignorial right was waived and, to make a long story shorter, a first sub, an impetuous, squat and sweaty standby led old Olga to the kitchen where, tugging at his zip, he tried to have her half way on-and-off the Sir Basil Wedgewood kitchen table. It was then of course that Madame Standby, his good wife, made an unfortunate and untimely entrance—unfortunate for herself that is. For she was incapable of throwing more than a look of outrage in such a circumstance. For which silent pacifism she received a puck in the eye from her hubby, the Lord of the flies. Meanwhile, harmony is continuing at the party proper. Our host still smiling and showing his fillings, his famous hand still favouring the lucky Sam. It was then I saw old Olga returning from her domestic adventure and I knew by the look she threw our way that her party piece was coming. You know it, you know it, Har, as well as anyone. 'People—people—I hate them—Just look at them.'

HARRY   'Haven't you seen them riding bicycles?'

FRANCISCO   That's it. Of course our host is clocking all these new developments too, and the further development a moment later of Madame Standby's reappearance from the kitchen, her eye already swelling up. And to follow this, the re-entry of her randy spouse, who was now, for reasons best known to himself, pretending to be chewing gum. Well, that did it. Well, it must have. Because it was then, suddenly, in mid-anecdote, that the famous favouring hand was withdrawn, and the deep rich resonant voice said sternly down at Sam, 'I'm afraid I must ask you to leave.' 'Pardon?' said Sam. From his vantage point he had been clocking nothing, so his amazement was clearly under-standable. 'Pardon?' he said again, and I thought he was going to faint. 'Leave, leave, leave!' screamed the great man shrilly, revealing that the deep rich reson-ance all along was falsetto, and was now reverting to the leopard spots of its natural strident, vibrant alto. And, simultaneously as I'm seeing, out of the corner of my eye, the randy Monsieur Standby hurrying 'cross the crowded room bent on doing me a damage, I got a puck in the back from another quarter which sent me sprawling towards our host. 'Just a moment, please'—I was very polite—but the next thing, I was

looking at a fistful of my hair in the hand that could
turn an artist into a cult. Nor could the great man
himself believe the sight of the fistful of my hair—so
what was his reaction?—but to attempt to get another
and another. (HARRY *laughs*) Enjoying it so far, Har?
In short, it was a vicious intellectual do. Actually, it
was Sam who cleared the space which allowed me to
pull free and see three heroes paw and grapple with
old Olga, lift her off her feet—their excited arms and
hands were to-and-fro her clutch—and bear her out
the screaming door. Everyone was excited. They would
not of course touch Sam, and for this very reason he
was to-and-fro—particularly the screaming jilly-journalists—kicking them mercilessly in their fast-growing
hysterical shins, and causing spaces. Actually, it was
by means of one of these spaces that I made my
escape, leaving—Mea Culpa!—little Sam behind.
Well, they would have killed *me*! They would! They
were intellectuals and therefore only half-wide. They
could kill you, so little do they know about it all. They
could really hurt you. But eventually they got Sam
out too. With walking sticks they did it. Not to beat
him, no! As I said they were loath to even touch him.
Loath to! To knock him. Hook his little legs, knock,
haul, prod—encourage him to leave. Hmm? What a
regrettable *volte-face* for civilization, I said to myself
a thousand times, and did not God, through his only
begotten son, his *only* son—because they had only the
one—redeem us from all this kind of thing. Could I
have a drink, Har?

HARRY (*Taking bottle to* FRANCISCO) Y'see? Y'see?

FRANCISCO Have one yourself, Har.

HARRY Without me you are nothing. (*Gives bottle to*
FRANCISCO)

FRANCISCO Are you quoting Scripture now?

HARRY You were being punished.

FRANCISCO Oh?

HARRY And soon you will be punished more.

FRANCISCO By you?

HARRY Yes, by me. And then by God. God found evil among
the angels and he didn't spare them, so what will he
do with you?

FRANCISCO So proud, Har, so righteous! What makes you so sure
of yourself? Time and time again, people have been

caught out. How often have you been told how, perhaps in a simple conversation such as this, such a man was stabbed, how such a man fell down and broke his neck, how another never rose from his game of poker? How such a woman killed herself. Hmm? I would have imagined that at this stage you would be saying, what is the point of all this to me. Hmm? (*He is handing the bottle down to* HARRY)

HARRY . . .No—no, you keep it, old boy.

FRANCISCO No, you keep it, old boy. (HARRY, *unsure, takes the bottle, then holds it up to* FRANCISCO *again*) No, you keep it. I haven't finished yet. (*To* MAUDIE) Sorry for the deviation, love. What a night of adventure! And all the time I knew—I knew—I knew—I knew, I knew we had not been paid!

HARRY You didn't get paid!

FRANCISCO No. But the pain of that thought, Harry. My honour —*my* honour!—exposed and scalding me. But my head would have none of it, and had already told my honour that it could not afford its pride. So, there we were, we three on the outside, looking at the cream-white luxury of that closed apartment door. Olga . . . Yes, contrary to what some people thought, I had a great regard, and affection, for old Olga.

HARRY What?

FRANCISCO (*Savagely*) Yes Har? (HARRY *mutters something*) What, Har?

HARRY I'm not a fool, Francisco.

FRANCISCO (*Nods, agreeing*) Olga was trembling, rather sexily I thought, her raven hair in rather lovely disarray, and kept hissing with passionate intensity the one word, cunts, repeatedly at a spot on the door. And Sam, Har— (*Harshly*) Har!

HARRY Oh, yes?

FRANCISCO Sam, also understandably agitated, but making as little constructive sense as Olga, was calling for our concerted effort to 'kick the fucking door down, man, and take the fucking lot of them.' Well, I went to the letterbox, sir, pushed open the flap, and called out the simple message, 'Our money, our money'. I could see them in the hall. What a ripple of excitement was now running through that party! What existentialism! And they called in urgent whispers for the host. I saw the great man appear and with a flourishing biro write us out a cheque on the hall's Sir Basil Wedgewood cheque-book table. I saw his adam's apple bob twice, and take the fucking lot of them'. Well, I went to the kept blowing on the biro-written cheque as he came to the waiting letterbox. He posted me the cheque with eyes cast down—like a Christian, Har—and said 'Be off with you, my man, at once or I shall have the fuzz here in a thrice'. Well, Olga grabbed the cheque to see if we were to be short-changed. But no! It was written out for forty-five, written and printed. Not the thirty nicker we'd agreed upon, but fifteen nicker extra. It wasn't a mistake. But as Olga said, why not twenty extra if he wanted to be generous, why not short-change us if he wanted to be a man? If an apology, why not the rounder figure, fifty? Or, as Olga said, is fifteen, three fivers, the standard sum for an insult to three persons? Or is fifteen the figure of an apology for the half man and the phony? Or, in that kind of contingency, as Olga said, is that the sum of Christian charity and amendment? How old Olga wrestled with the psychological apologetics of that one! How that detail preyed on old Olga's mind . . . to the end.

HARRY (*Taking bottle to him*) And what did you do?

FRANCISCO I beg your pardon? (FRANCISCO *is frowning, incredulous of* HARRY'S *unwillingness or inability to get the message*)

HARRY Did you take it?

FRANCISCO I thought the tragic ending to my story was lucid.

HARRY I wouldn't have taken it! I wouldn't, I wouldn't! . . . What? . . . Well I would have . . .

FRANCISCO Yeh?

HARRY Well, that's very—y'know? That's very interesting. And what am I expected to do about it? Is it my affair? (*Shouts*) It's got nothing to do with me!

FRANCISCO Shh!

HARRY What?

FRANCISCO (*Indicates that somebody outside might hear them. Then*) It has.

HARRY What? What did you come here for, Francisco? Francisco, I know you! Do you know what's been going on in my mind for you? (*His knife clutched in his hand*) And you, Olga, and Sam, I can't take any more of you! You made your filthy bed, now sleep in it. That's a proverb, isn't it? Well then! You—you three make a right—a right Holy Family—A right-looking Holy Family, Maudie! You should see them sometimes. Polluting, poisoning the air. So—y'know? —If you'll drink up—If you'd care to drink up, you can be—Toddle along.

FRANCISCO Oh no.

HARRY Yes! You can go, leave!

FRANCISCO I've no intention of going!

HARRY Stop! I said you can go now.

FRANCISCO I'm not going traipsing all the way back to Paxton Street —

HARRY I'm letting you go!

FRANCISCO At this hour of the morning.

HARRY Francisco!

FRANCISCO Are you a Catholic, Maud?

HARRY Francisco!

FRANCISCO Maud —

HARRY No, she's not.

FRANCISCO What?

HARRY She's not, she's not!—Why should she?—Why should she?

FRANCISCO I agree—How I agree! Don't I agree! What a poxy con the lot is!

HARRY (*Wearily*) Francisco.

MAUDIE I think my mam were.

FRANCISCO And so was Olga, Maud. And so was Olga, Har. And I was a Catholic for the F.B.I. But what a con! I knew you were only joking about being happy here. What an industry! The great middle-man industry! I had occasion the other day to negotiate with them, not too successfully, for a holy grave. But what a poxy con! All Christianity! All those predators that have been mass-produced out of the loneliness and isolation of people, with standard collars stamped on! And what do they give back? Those coonics! They're like black candles, not giving, but each one drawing a little more light out of the world. (HARRY *makes some movement. A weary plea to* FRANCISCO: FRANCISCO *misinterprets the move and swings the candlestick viciously*) Oh, they could kill you—Oh they can really hurt you, so little do they know about it all! Hopping on their rubber-soled formulas and equations! Selling their product: Jesus. Weaving their theological cobwebs, doing their theological sums! Black on the outside but, underneath, their bodies swathed in bandages—bandages steeped in ointments, preservatives and holy oils!—Half mummified torsos like great thick bandaged pricks! Founded in blood, continued in blood, crusaded in blood, inquisitioned in blood, divided in blood—And *they* tell *us* that Christ lives! Nothing to live for but to die! They arrive at their temporary sated state, these violence-mongering furies, and start verily wanking themselves in pleasurable swoons of pacifism, forgetting their own history. And then insist—Insist!—that Jesus, total man, life-enhancing man, Jesus!— should be the only killer of life! Die to self? I doze father, I doze! Peace, Ecumenism? —I doze, father, I doze! They cannot agree among themselves on the first three words of the Our Father Get the police in!—(*He laughs*) Get heavy mounted police in with heavy mounted batons and disperse them, rout them, get them back from the round tables before they start the third and final world war we've all been dreading!

HARRY (*Again determined*) Come down!

FRANCISCO *laughs and swings the candlestick viciously again. The clock chimes two.*

FRANCISCO I have a dream, I have a dream! The day is coming, the second coming, the final judgment, the not too distant future, before that simple light of man: when Jesus, Man, total man, will call to his side the goats— 'Come ye blessed!' Yea, call to his side all those rakish, dissolute, suicidal, fornicating goats, taken in adultery and what-have-you. And proclaim to the coonics, blush for shame, you blackguards, be off with you, you wretches, depart from me ye accursed complicated affliction! And that, my dear brother and sister, is my dream, my hope, my vision and my belief. (*He comes down from the pulpit and kneels on one knee before* HARRY) Your blessing, Har.

HARRY (*Knife in his hand*) Would you—would you die for your belief?

FRANCISCO (*Indicates that he is already kneeling*) You kill for yours? (*Short pause. Rising*) Then put away your sword. Where do I sleep? Just point to the spot and

I'll flop there. We might as well get a few hours before
we're evicted.

HARRY (*Feebly*) What have you to tell me, Francisco?

FRANCISCO Aw, you're not that slow on the uptake, Har. Where's
the loo? In here, Maud, is it?

MAUDIE *leads* FRANCISCO *off.*

HARRY (*Calls after them*) It's Teresa I'm talking about,
Teresa! Not Olga . . . 'Everyone to blame but you,
Har?' I'm not in the wrong. (*To lamp*) Do you
believe what he says? That muck? All that insinua-
tion? I'm not in the wrong. Did he sneak my wife
or didn't he? Well then! Did Teresa die or didn't
she? . . . Are you dumb, are you dumb? I was one
of the best of sports, anyone will tell you that. I was
a famous man. So—y'see? . . . I don't *feel* I'm in the
wrong . . . And once, in the morning actually, towards
the end, little girl—y'know?—got out of her cot, out
of her cot, all by herself—I was very surprised—some
music was playing, and danced, actually. Danced.
(*He has been weaving his hands in the air, vaguely
balletic, reminiscent of a child*) Of course Olga was a
dancer too. Not a very good one, of course. (*Recon-
siders*) Well, perhaps above the average. She's gone
and left him. Olga—y'know? That's what I think.
That's all . . . (*He is near tears*) Are you dumb . . .
I believe . . . Help.

> *Music has come up and the lights are now fading a
> little (to suggest the passage of time).* MAUDIE *has
> entered to stand beside* HARRY *with an armful of
> cushions.* HARRY *rises wearily to lay the confessional
> horizontal on the floor.* FRANCISCO *from the back-
> ground coming to his assistance . . .*

SCENE TWO

MAUDIE *is asleep in one of the three compartments of the
confessional.* FRANCISCO *is in another compartment, sitting up,
rolling a cigarette.* HARRY *is sitting listlessly in a pew. It is nearly
three a.m.*

51

FRANCISCO   (*Whispering*) Harry? Harry? . . . Maud? . . . Maud?
(MAUDIE *is waking up.* FRANCISCO *chuckling and lighting his cigarette*) Give me a child until he is seven, they say, and then you can have him back. Ask me to say the Confiteor. I can't. I've forgotten it. I've beaten them . . . You're praying to a dying horse here, Har.

HARRY   And what are you doing? Kicking him?

FRANCISCO   Not bad. But you agree the horse is dying?

HARRY   No. I don't agree with you.

MAUDIE   You don't get children back. They're gone. You get other ones.

FRANCISCO   Yeh, they're gone. And there's no one on earth to tell you where they've gone. And there's no one to bless you. And, worse, there's no one to curse you.

MAUDIE   There's forgiveness.

FRANCISCO   What? You're free tomorrow, Maud, I'm free too. Know what I mean?

MAUDIE   I'm going home to gran. And to grandad. (MAUDIE *settles back to sleep in her compartment. Pause*)

FRANCISCO   Teresa, Olga, and Stephen. Harry, Olga is dead. Two days after that last gig. An overdose. OD. They talked about it in shorthand (*The clock chimes three.* HARRY *reacts to the clock. He gets the replacement candle for the sanctuary lamp through the following*) A couple of days later Sam packed his bag. He got taken back into the circus. I tried them too but they wouldn't have me—(*Chuckles*) for some reason or other . . . Remember the talking we used to do in bed in the old days?

HARRY   Don't remember.

FRANCISCO   The little pad we used to doss in?

HARRY   No.

FRANCISCO   That pad: one big bed. Nothing queer, Maud.

HARRY   Oh, no.

FRANCISCO   Hmm?

HARRY   Nothing like that—y'know?

FRANCISCO   I think she's asleep. We used to sit up in bed half the night talking.

HARRY   Discussing, actually.

FRANCISCO   Yeh.

HARRY   We didn't always agree.

FRANCISCO   But we had a laugh.

HARRY   Excuse for just a second, old boy. (HARRY *replaces the candle in the sanctuary lamp. He returns and sits on a corner of the confessional. They have talked themselves sober*) I disagree.

FRANCISCO Yeh?

HARRY Where you go when you die.

FRANCISCO Yeh?

HARRY Silhouettes.

FRANCISCO Yeh?

HARRY The soul—y'know?—like a silhouette. And when you die it moves out into . . . slow-moving mists of space and time. Awake in oblivion actually. And it moves out from the world to take its place in the silent outer wall of eternity. The wall that keeps all those moving mists of time and space together.

FRANCISCO But there must be an outer wall there already.

HARRY Oh yes. Shell-like.

FRANCISCO But the wall is built already, if it's an eternal wall.

HARRY Oh yes.

FRANCISCO So what's to be done with the new soul—silhouettes that arrive? (*Chuckles*) Stack them in sheds.

HARRY No.

FRANCISCO Yeh?

HARRY Stack them, softly, like clouds, in a corner of space, where they must wait for a time. Until they are needed.

FRANCISCO Yeh?

HARRY And if a hole comes in one of the silhouettes already in that wall, a new one is called for, and implanted on the damaged one. And whose silhouette is the new one? The father's. The father of the damaged one. Or the mother's sometimes. Or a brother's, or a sweetheart's. Loved ones. That's it. And one is implanted on the other. And the merging—y'know? Merging?—merging of the silhouettes is true union. Union forever of loved ones, actually.

FRANCISCO I don't know if I agree.

HARRY Oh yes?

FRANCISCO But it's certainly as good, better, than anything they've come up with.

HARRY Oh yes.

FRANCISCO There was one thing that used to appeal to me. When I was young, Har, do you know what I used to think of every night? The pain of the thought! That I hadn't died before they got to baptize me.

HARRY Oh yes.

FRANCISCO Because if you were baptized you could get to heaven alright, but you couldn't get to Limbo.

HARRY   You were disbarred.

FRANCISCO   Yeh. Baptism—the passport to heaven—disbarred you. And contrary to what they thought, I thought—same as any other sensible baby would—that Limbo was the place to get to. It was tropical really. Imagine, the only snag to Limbo was that you never got to see the face of God. Imagine that. Now, what baby, I ask you, gives a burp about the face of God. No, the only thing that babies feared was the hand of God, that could hold your little baby body in his fist, before dipping you into the red hot coals of hell. Then take you out again and hold you up before his un-shaved and slobbering chin, before dipping you again, this time into the damp black heat of purgatory. Experimenting. Playing with Himself. Wondering which type of heat to cook you on.

HARRY   Oh yes?

FRANCISCO   No, babies are wide, Har, babies are shrewd. Well, they aren't fools. And they are grossly abused in the great trade-union of Baptism. Oh but Limbo, Har, Limbo! With just enough light rain to keep the place lush green, the sunshine and red flowers, and the thousands and thousands of other fat babies sitting under the trees, gurgling and laughing and eating bananas . . . The pain of not having died.

HARRY   Any thoughts on madness, Francisco? . . . No?

FRANCISCO   No. I don't think it's a refuge. Do you?

HARRY   No, actually. No.

FRANCISCO   But that soul-silhouette theory isn't bad. I mean, it's a starting point, you can be developing on it.

HARRY   Indeed.

FRANCISCO   What time have we to be up and out of here?

HARRY   Seven.

FRANCISCO   (*He looks at* HARRY *for a moment*) We'll go together, right? (HARRY *nods. Sleepily*) It's quite an adventure though. It isn't half bad down here. (*Yawns, settling back to sleep*) Oh my God I am heartily sorry for having offended thee and I . . . See? I can't remember. I've beaten them. Goodnight, Har.

Pause

HARRY   Y'know!

54

22-25